Hippobottymus

written by
STEVE SMALLMAN

illustrated by **ADA GREY**

LITTLE TIGER PRESS
London

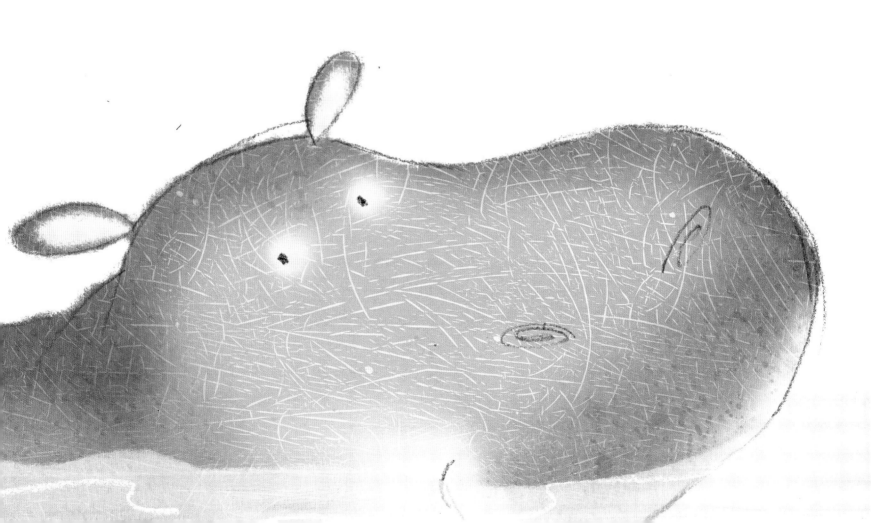

A mouse sat down by a bubbling creek –
The creek went **bubble** and
the mouse went squeak!

Squeak, squeak, bubble, bubble,
squeak, squeak, squeak.
Squeak, squeak,
bubble, bubble,
squeak, squeak,
squeak!

A little bird tweeted,
"What a
GREAT song!
And if you don't
mind, I'll sing along!"

"Wait!" yelled Centipede. "You need a beat!" So he tapped out a rhythm with his tappity feet...

Tip-tap-a-tippy-tappy, tweet-tweet-tweet,

Squeak, squeak, bubble, bubble, squeak, Squeak, **Squeak!**

Monkey heard the music and he cried, "**Woo-hoo!** That sounds so **cool**, can I join in too?"

Warthog said,
"I'VE GOT A MUSICAL BUM!"
Then he banged on his bottom like a big bass drum...

tweet-tweet-tweet,

Squeak, squeak,
bubble, bubble,
squeak, Squeak,
Squeak!

Then
along came a
great
BIG
croc

odile.

He listened to the music and it made him smile!

He reached in his pocket and he took out a bone...

...Then he played on his teeth like a xylophone!

PLINK PLINK PLINK-A-PLONK! PLINKETTY-PLOO!

BOOM-BA-DA-BOOM-BOOM!
Ooh, ooh, ooh!
Tip-tap-a-tippy-tappy,
tweet-tweet-tweet.
Squeak, squeak, bubble, bubble,
squeak, squeak,
squeak!

Well they danced and they played till a quarter to four,
Then they all flopped down in a heap on the floor.
"Wow!" cheered Mouse. "Now, wasn't that fun?
You guys ROCKED! Hooray! Well done!"

"Thanks!" they cried. "We helped, it's true,
But the person we should
thank is..."

"Excuse me?" Mouse said. "But what did you do?
Monkey was the one who went **ooh, ooh, ooh!**
Centipede **tapped** with his **tappity** feet,
And this little bird went tweet, tweet, tweet."

"Warthog banged on his musical bum –
It went BOOM-BA-DA-BOOM!
like a big bass drum!
Crocodile played plink, plinketty-ploo,

Hippo said,
"Well, **I** ate beans this week...
My bottom made the **bubbles**
in the **bubbling** creek!"